POPPLETON
HAS FUN

CYNTHIA RYLANT

POPPLETON

HAS FUN

BOOK SEVEN

Illustrated by
MARK TEAGUE

SCHOLASTIC INC.
New York Toronto London Auckland Sydney
Mexico City New Delhi Hong Kong

To Robert and Christina
M. T.

ISBN 0-590-84841-0

This book is being published simultaneously in hardcover by
the Blue Sky Press.

Text copyright © 2000 by Cynthia Rylant
Illustrations copyright © 2000 by Mark Teague
All rights reserved.
Published by Scholastic Inc.
SCHOLASTIC and associated logos are trademarks
and/or registered trademarks of Scholastic Inc.

12 11 10 9 8 7 6 5 4 3 2   0 1 2 3 4 5/0

Printed in the United States of America   23

Designed by Kathleen Westray

First Scholastic Trade paperback printing, October 2000

CONTENTS

THE MOVIE

Poppleton decided one day to see a movie.

He asked his neighbor Cherry Sue
to go, but she couldn't.
She was stretching.

"Tell me how it is!" she said,
stretching out long.

Poppleton went to the movie alone.

He had never been to a movie alone.

This might be fun, he thought.

He wouldn't
have to share
any popcorn.

He wouldn't
have to share
any candy.

No one would
ask for a drink
of his pop.

Poppleton was very cheerful
when he got to the movie theater.
He ordered a giant popcorn.

He ordered a giant candy bar.

He ordered a giant pop.

Then the movie started.

At first Poppleton loved being alone
with all of his movie snacks.
But then a scary part came.
Poppleton was scared,
and there was no one to be with!

Then a funny part came,

and there was no one to laugh with!

Then, worst of all, a sad part came.

Poppleton sobbed and sobbed.

But there was no one to ask for a tissue.

When the movie ended,
Poppleton had a runny nose
and too many snacks.
He went to see Cherry Sue.

"How was it?" she asked.

Poppleton told her about the scary part.

Cherry Sue was scared, too!

Poppleton told her about the funny part.
Cherry Sue laughed and laughed!

Poppleton told her about the sad part.
Cherry Sue filled ten tissues with tears.

Poppleton gave Cherry Sue
his leftover movie snacks.
"I am never going to a movie
alone again," said Poppleton.

And he didn't!

THE QUILT

Poppleton and his neighbor
Cherry Sue went to a fair.
There they saw quilts.

The quilts had pictures on them

and names

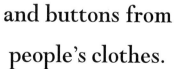

and buttons from
people's clothes.

"We should make our own quilt,"
Poppleton said to Cherry Sue.
"What fun!" said Cherry Sue.
"We will ask Hudson and Fillmore
to help," said Poppleton.
"Perfect!" said Cherry Sue.

Poppleton called his friends.

"We are making a quilt on Saturday,"
Poppleton told Hudson. "Can you come?"

"Sure!" said Hudson.

Poppleton called Fillmore.

"We are making a quilt on Saturday,"
said Poppleton. "Can you come?"

"Certainly!" said Fillmore.

On Saturday everyone
met at Poppleton's house.
Fillmore had some
old shirts.

Hudson had some

old trousers.

Poppleton had some old curtains.

And Cherry Sue had
a bucket of buttons.

"Let's sew!" said Poppleton.

While they were sewing,
they all told stories.
Fillmore told them about the time
he saw a double rainbow.

Hudson told them about the time
he jumped out of a plane.

Cherry Sue told them about the time
she dyed her hair green.

And Poppleton told them about the time
he lived on a houseboat.

At the end of the day,
the quilt was finished.
And it had all of their stories!

The friends were proud.
They decided to take turns
keeping the quilt.

Poppleton got it in summer.

Fillmore got it in fall.

Cherry Sue got it in winter.

And Hudson got it in spring.

Every season of every year,

someone was sleeping under stories.

THE SOAK

Poppleton liked nothing better
than soaking in a hot tub.

When he was tired, he would say,
"I need a soak."

When he was worried, he would say,
"I need a soak."

Even when he felt happy,

a soak made him happier.

When Poppleton soaked,
he liked to use good bath stuff.

He used a little lavender.

He used a little lemon.

He used a little silky milk.

When he got out, he smelled very good.

One day Poppleton ran out of
good bath stuff.
He walked over to Cherry Sue's.
"Do you have any good bath stuff?"
Poppleton asked.
"I don't take baths," said Cherry Sue.
"I shower."

"You don't soak?" asked Poppleton.

"No," said Cherry Sue.

"No lavender?" asked Poppleton.

"No."

"No lemon?" asked Poppleton.

"No."

"No silky milk?" asked Poppleton.

"No silky milk," said Cherry Sue.

"Hmmm," said Poppleton. "Do you
have *anything* I can soak in?"

"Let's see," said Cherry Sue.

"How about some blueberries?"

"I'll smell like a cobbler," said Poppleton.

"How about some cinnamon?"
said Cherry Sue.

"I'll smell like a pie," said Poppleton.

"How about some vanilla?"
said Cherry Sue.
"I'll smell like...say, are you
hungry?" said Poppleton.
"I am now," said Cherry Sue.
"Let's go," said Poppleton.

Poppleton missed his soak that day.
But it was okay.

He was very happy smelling
like a banana split!